THE MINIATURE MOTHER GOOSE

ILLUSTRATED BY
BLANCHE FISHER WRIGHT

Ernest Benn
TONBRIDGE

This edition first published 1983 by
Ernest Benn Ltd., Sovereign Way,
Tonbridge, KENT TN9 1RW
Copyright 1916 by Rand McNally & Company
Renewal copyright 1944 by
Rand McNally & Company.

ISBN 0 510 00141 6
Printed in Hong Kong
by South China Printing Co.

Lisa
Christmas
1987

INDEX

LITTLE JACK HORNER

Little Jack Horner
Sat in the corner,
    Eating of Christmas pie:
He put in his thumb,
    And pulled out a plum,
And said, "What a good boy am I!"

THE ROBIN

The north wind doth blow,
And we shall have snow,
And what will poor robin do then,
     Poor thing?
He'll sit in a barn,
And keep himself warm,
And hide his head under his wing,
     Poor thing!

POLLY AND SUKEY

Polly, put the kettle on,
Polly, put the kettle on,
Polly, put the kettle on,
    And let's drink tea.

Sukey, take it off again,
Sukey, take it off again,
Sukey, take it off again,
    They're all gone away.

OH, DEAR!

Dear, dear! what can the matter be?
Two old women got up in an apple-
tree;
One came down, and the other
stayed till Saturday.

THE MAN IN OUR TOWN

There was a man in our town,
    And he was wondrous wise,
He jumped into a bramble bush,
    And scratched out both his
      eyes;
But when he saw his eyes were out,
    With all his might and main,
He jumped into another bush,
    And scratched 'em in again.

THE FIRST OF MAY

The fair maid who, the first of May,
Goes to the fields at break of day,
And washes in dew from the haw-
    thorn-tree,
Will ever after handsome be.

CAESAR'S SONG

Bow-wow-wow!

Whose dog art thou?

Little Tom Tinker's dog,

Bow-wow-wow!

WHY MAY NOT I LOVE JOHNNY?

Johnny shall have a new bonnet,
  And Johnny shall go to the fair,
And Johnny shall have a blue ribbon
  To tie up his bonny brown hair.

And why may not I love Johnny?
  And why may not Johnny
    love me?
And why may not I love Johnny
  As well as another body?

And here's a leg for a stocking,
  And here's a foot for a shoe,
And he has a kiss for his daddy,
  And two for his mammy, I trow.

And why may not I love Johnny?
  And why may not Johnny love
    me?
And why may not I love Johnny
  As well as another body?

BOBBY SNOOKS

Little Bobby Snooks was fond of
his books,
And loved by his usher and master;
But naughty Jack Spry, he got a
black eye,
And carries his nose in a plaster.

TOMMY SNOOKS

As Tommy Snooks and Bessy
    Brooks
    Were walking out one Sunday,
Says Tommy Snooks to Bessy
    Brooks,
    "Wilt marry me on Monday?"

DANCE TO YOUR DADDIE

Dance to your daddie,
My bonnie laddie;
Dance to your daddie, my bonnie
    lamb;
You shall get a fishy,
On a little dishy;
You shall get a fishy, when the boat
    comes home.

THE MAN OF DERBY

A little old man of Derby,
How do you think he served me?
He took away my bread and cheese,
And that is how he served me.

HANDY PANDY

Handy Pandy, Jack-a-dandy,
Loves plum cake and sugar candy.
He bought some at a grocer's shop,
And out he came, hop, hop, hop!

THE OLD WOMAN OF GLOUCESTER

There was an old woman of
    Gloucester,
Whose parrot two guineas it cost
    her,
    But its tongue never ceasing,
    Was vastly displeasing
To the talkative woman of
    Gloucester.

WILLY, WILLY

Willy, Willy Wilkin
Kissed the maids a-milking,
    Fa, la, la!
And with his merry daffing
He set them all a-laughing,
    Ha, ha, ha!

A SURE TEST

If you are to be a gentleman,
  As I suppose you'll be,
You'll neither laugh nor smile,
  For a tickling of the knee.

COFFEE AND TEA

Molly, my sister and I fell out,
And what do you think it was all
about?
She loved coffee and I loved tea,
And that was the reason we couldn't
agree.

DAFFODILS

Daffy-down-dilly has come to town
In a yellow petticoat and a green
gown.

LITTLE GIRL AND QUEEN

"Little girl, little girl, where have
    you been?"
"Gathering roses to give to the
    Queen."
"Little girl, little girl, what gave
    she you?"
"She gave me a diamond as big as
    my shoe."

BAA, BAA, BLACK SHEEP

Baa, baa, black sheep,
Have you any wool?
Yes, marry, have I,
Three bags full;

One for my master,
One for my dame,
But none for the little boy
Who cries in the lane.

TOMMY TITTLEMOUSE

Little Tommy Tittlemouse
Lived in a little house;
He caught fishes
In other men's ditches.

JACK AND JILL

Jack and Jill went up the hill,
  To fetch a pail of water;
Jack fell down, and broke his crown,
  And Jill came tumbling after.

I'LL TELL YOU A STORY

I'll tell you a story
About Jack-a-Nory:
And now my story's begun.
I'll tell you another
About his brother:
And now my story is done.

A STRANGE OLD WOMAN

There was an old woman, and what
    do you think?
She lived upon nothing but victuals
    and drink;
Victuals and drink were the chief
    of her diet,
And yet this old woman could
    never be quiet.

THE FARMER AND THE RAVEN

A farmer went trotting upon his
gray mare,
Bumpety, bumpety, bump!
With his daughter behind him so
rosy and fair,
Lumpety, lumpety, lump!

A raven cried croak! and they all
tumbled down,
Bumpety, bumpety, bump!
The mare broke her knees, and the
farmer his crown,
Lumpety, lumpety, lump!

The mischievous raven flew laugh-
ing away,
Bumpety, bumpety, bump!
And vowed he would serve them
the same the next day,
Lumpety, lumpety lump!

THE ROBINS

A robin and a robin's son
Once went to town to buy a bun.
They couldn't decide on plum or
     plain,
And so they went back home again.

PANCAKE DAY

Great A, little a,
This is pancake day;
Toss the ball high,
Throw the ball low,
Those that come after
May sing heigh-ho!

TWO PIGEONS

I had two pigeons bright and gay,
They flew from me the other day.
What was the reason they did go?
I cannot tell, for I do not know.

BANDY LEGS

As I was going to sell my eggs
I met a man with bandy legs,
Bandy legs and crooked toes;
I tripped up his heels, and he
fell on his nose.

THE LITTLE MOPPET

I had a little moppet,
I put it in my pocket,
And fed it with corn and hay.
There came a proud beggar.
And swore he should have her;
And stole my little moppet away.

IF WISHES WERE HORSES

If wishes were horses, beggars would
ride.

If turnips were watches, I would
wear one by my side.
And if "ifs" and "ands"
Were pots and pans,
There'd be no work for tinkers!

LITTLE MAID

"Little maid, pretty maid, whither
    goest thou?"
"Down in the forest to milk my
    cow."
'Shall I go with thee?"   "No, not
    now;
When I send for thee, then come
    thou."

SING, SING

Sing, sing, what shall I
    sing?

Cat's run away with the
    pudding-string!

Do, do, what shall I
    do?

The cat has bitten it
    quite in two.

MY KITTEN

Hey, my kitten, my kitten,
  And hey, my kitten, my deary!
Such a sweet pet as this
  Was neither far nor neary.

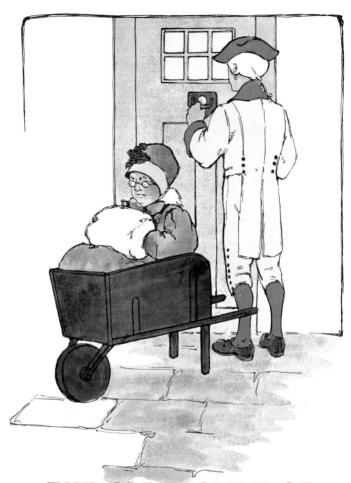

THE OLD WOMAN OF HARROW

There was an old woman of Harrow,
Who visited in a wheelbarrow;
And her servant before,
Knocked loud at each door,
To announce the old woman of Harrow

THE GIRL IN THE LANE

The girl in the lane, that couldn't
    speak plain,
  Cried, "Gobble, gobble, gobble":
The man on the hill that couldn't
    stand still,
  Went hobble hobble, hobble.

A LITTLE MAN

There was a little man, and he had
    a little gun,
    And his bullets were made of
    lead, lead, lead;

He went to the brook, and saw a
little duck,
And shot it right through the
head, head, head.

He carried it home to his old wife
Joan,
And bade her a fire to make,
make, make.

To roast the little duck he had shot
in the brook,
And he'd go and fetch the drake,
drake, drake.

The drake was a-swimming with
his curly tail;
The little man made it his mark,
mark, mark.

He let off his gun, but he fired
too soon,
And the drake flew away with a
quack, quack, quack.

A B C

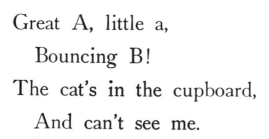

Great A, little a,
   Bouncing B!
The cat's in the cupboard,
   And can't see me.

ONE TO TEN

1, 2, 3, 4, 5!
I caught a hare alive;
6, 7, 8, 9, 10!
I let her go again.

THE MAN WHO HAD NAUGHT

There was a man and he had naught,
    And robbers came to rob him;
He crept up to the chimney pot,
    And then they thought they
      had him.

But he got down on t'other side,
    And then they could not find
      him;
He ran fourteen miles in fifteen days,
    And never looked behind him.

PINS

See a pin and pick it up,
All the day you'll have good luck.
See a pin and let it lay,
Bad luck you'll have all the day.

49

PIPPEN HILL

As I was going up Pippen Hill,
  Pippen Hill was dirty;
There I met a pretty Miss,
  And she dropped me a
  curtsy.

Little Miss, pretty Miss,
  Blessings light upon you;
If I had half-a-crown a day,
  I'd spend it all upon you.

MARY'S CANARY

Mary had a pretty bird,
    Feathers bright and yellow,
Slender legs—upon my word
    He was a pretty fellow!
The sweetest note he always sung,
    Which much delighted Mary.
She often, where the cage was hung,
    Sat hearing her canary.

BEES

A swarm of bees in May
Is worth a load of hay;
A swarm of bees in June
Is worth a silver spoon;
A swarm of bees in July
Is not worth a fly.

ABOUT THE BUSH

About the bush, Willie,
    About the beehive,
About the bush, Willie,
    I'll meet thee alive.

A SUNSHINY SHOWER

A sunshiny shower
Won't last half an hour.

THE CLOCK

There's a neat little clock,—
    In the schoolroom it stands,—
And it points to the time
    With its two little hands.

And may we, like the clock,
    Keep a face clean and bright,
With hands ever ready
    To do what is right.

THERE WAS AN OLD WOMAN

There was an old woman who lived
    in a shoe.
She had so many children she
    didn't know what to do.
She gave them some broth without
    any bread.
She whipped them all soundly and
    put them to bed.

THE GREEDY MAN

The greedy man is he who sits
    And bites bits out of plates,
Or else takes up an almanac
    And gobbles all the dates.

THE MAN OF BOMBAY

There was a fat man of Bombay,

Who was smoking one sunshiny day;

When a bird called a snipe

Flew away with his pipe,

Which vexed the fat man of Bombay

THE DERBY RAM

As I was going to Derby all on a
    market-day,
I met the finest ram, sir, that ever
    was fed upon hay;
Upon hay, upon hay, upon hay;

I met the finest ram, sir, that ever
    was fed upon hay.
This ram was fat behind, sir; this
    ram was fat before;
This ram was ten yards round, sir;
    indeed, he was no more;
    No more, no more, no more;
This ram was ten yards round, sir;
    indeed, he was no more.
The horns that grew on his head, sir,
    they were so wondrous high,
As I've been plainly told, sir, they
    reached up to the sky.
    The sky, the sky, the sky;
As I've been plainly told, sir, they
    reached up to the sky.

The tail that grew from his back, sir,
    was six yards and an ell;
And it was sent to Derby to toll the
    market bell;
    The bell, the bell, the bell;
And it was sent to Derby to toll
    the market bell.

THE DUSTY MILLER

Margaret wrote a letter,
Sealed it with her finger,
Threw it in the dam
For the dusty miller.
Dusty was his coat,
Dusty was the siller,
Dusty was the kiss
I'd from the dusty miller.
If I had my pockets
Full of gold and siller,
I would give it all
To my dusty miller.

INTERY, MINTERY

Intery, mintery, cutery corn,
Apple seed and apple thorn;
Wire, brier, limber-lock,
Five geese in a flock,
Sit and sing by a spring,
O-u-t, and in again.

A STAR

Higher than a house, higher
than a tree.
Oh! whatever can that be?

T'OTHER LITTLE TUNE

I won't be my father's Jack,
   I won't be my father's Jill;
I will be the fiddler's wife,
   And have music when I will.
      T'other little tune,
      T'other little tune,
      Prithee, Love, play me
      T'other little tune.

THE MERCHANTS OF LONDON

Hey diddle dinkety poppety pet,

The merchants of London they wear scarlet,

Silk in the collar and gold in the hem,

So merrily march the merchant men.

RAIN

Rain, rain, go to Spain,
And never come back again.

BLUE BELL BOY

I had a little boy,
And called him Blue Bell;
Gave him a little work,—
He did it very well.

I bade him go upstairs
To bring me a gold pin;
In coal scuttle fell he,
Up to his little chin.

He went to the garden
To pick a little sage;
He tumbled on his nose,
And fell into a rage.

He went to the cellar
To draw a little beer;
And quickly did return
To say there was none there.

THE OLD WOMAN UNDER A HILL

There was an old woman
Lived under a hill;
And if she's not gone,
She lives there still.

AS I WAS GOING ALONG

As I was going along, along,
A-singing a comical song, song, song,
The lane that I went was so long,
    long, long,
And the song that I sang was so
    long, long, long,
And so I went singing along.

TWO BIRDS

There were two birds sat on a stone,
    Fa, la, la, la, lal, de;
One flew away, and then there was
    one,
    Fa, la, la, la, lal, de;
The other bird flew after,
And then there was none,
    Fa, la, la, la, lal, de;
And so the stone, was left alone,
    Fa, la, la, la, lal, de.

THE MAN IN THE MOON

The Man in the Moon came tumbling
    down,

    And asked the way to Norwich;
He went by the south, and burnt his
    mouth

    With eating cold pease porridge.

SEE-SAW

See-saw, Margery Daw,
Sold her bed and lay upon straw.

THE CROOKED
SIXPENCE

There was a crooked man, and he
went a crooked mile,
He found a crooked sixpence be-
side a crooked stile;
He bought a crooked cat, which
caught a crooked mouse,
And they all lived together in a
little crooked house.

THREE BLIND MICE

Three blind mice! See how they run!
They all ran after the farmer's wife,
Who cut off their tails with a carv-
ing knife.
Did you ever see such a thing in
your life
As three blind mice?

THAT'S ALL

There was an old woman sat spinning,
And that's the first beginning;
She had a calf,
And that's half;
She took it by the tail,
And threw it over the wall,
And that's all!

I LOVE SIXPENCE

I love sixpence, a jolly, jolly sixpence,
  I love sixpence as my life;
I spent a penny of it, I spent a penny of it,
  I took a penny home to my wife.

THE WOMAN OF EXETER

There dwelt an old woman at Exeter;
When visitors came it sore vexed her,
    So for fear they should eat,
    She locked up all her meat,
This stingy old woman of Exeter.

BILLY, BILLY

"Billy, Billy, come and play,
While the sun shines bright as day."

"Yes, my Polly, so I will,
For I love to please you still."

"Billy, Billy, have you seen
Sam and Betsy on the green?"

"Yes, my Poll, I saw them pass,
Skipping o'er the new-mown grass."

"Billy, Billy, come along,
And I will sing a pretty song."

BUTTONS

Buttons, a farthing a pair!
Come, who will buy them of me?
They're round and sound and pretty,
And fit for girls of the city.
Come, who will buy them of me?
Buttons, a farthing a pair!

THE OLD WOMAN OF LEEDS

There was an old woman of Leeds,
Who spent all her time in good
       deeds;
    She worked for the poor
    Till her fingers were sore,
This pious old woman of Leeds!

THE MAN IN THE WILDERNESS

The man in the wilderness
    Asked me
How many strawberries
    Grew in the sea.
I answered him
    As I thought good,
As many as red herrings
    Grew in the wood.

WHISTLE

"Whistle, daughter, whistle;
    Whistle, daughter dear."
"I cannot whistle, mammy,
    I cannot whistle clear."
"Whistle, daughter, whistle;
    Whistle for a pound."
"I cannot whistle, mammy,
    I cannot make a sound."

BABY DOLLY

Hush, baby, my dolly, I pray you
    don't cry,
And I'll give you some bread, and
    some milk by-and-by;
Or perhaps you like custard, or,
    maybe, a tart,
Then to either you're welcome, with
    all my heart.

FIVE TOES

This little pig went to market;
This little pig stayed at home;
This little pig had roast beef;
This little pig had none;
This little pig said, "Wee, wee!
I can't find my way home."

THE CLEVER HEN

I had a little hen, the prettiest
ever seen,

She washed me the dishes and
kept the house clean;

She went to the mill to fetch me
　　some flour,
She brought it home in less than
　　an hour;
She baked me my bread, she
　　brewed me my ale,
She sat by the fire and told
　　many a fine tale.

TWEEDLE-DUM AND
TWEEDLE-DEE

Tweedle-dum and Tweedle-dee
　　Resolved to have a battle,
For Tweedle-dum said Tweedle-dee
　　Had spoiled his nice new rattle.

Just then flew by a monstrous crow,
　　As big as a tar barrel,
Which frightened both the heroes so,
　　They quite forgot their quarrel.

SULKY SUE

Here's Sulky Sue,
What shall we do?
Turn her face to the wall
Till she comes to.

SWAN

Swan, swan, over the sea;
Swim, swan, swim!
Swan, swan, back again;
Well swum, swan!

A MELANCHOLY SONG

Trip upon trenchers,

And dance upon dishes,

My mother sent me for some barm,
     some barm;

She bid me go lightly,

And come again quickly,

For fear the young men should do
     me some harm.

Yet didn't you see, yet didn't you
     see,

What naughty tricks they put upon
     me?

They broke my pitcher

   And spilt the water,

And huffed my mother,

   And chid her daughter,

And kissed my sister

   instead of me.

THE BALLOON

"What is the news of the day,
Good neighbour, I pray?"
"They say the balloon
Is gone up to the moon!"

THE FLYING PIG

Dickory, dickory, dare,
The pig flew up in the air;
The man in brown soon brought
   him down,

Dickory,
dickory,
dare.

CROSS PATCH

Cross patch, draw the latch,
    Sit by the fire and spin;
Take a cup and drink it up,
    Then call your neighbours in.

BESSY BELL AND
MARY GRAY

Bessy Bell and Mary Gray,
    They were two bonny lasses;
They built their house upon the lea,
    And covered it with rushes.

Bessy kept the garden gate,
    And Mary kept the pantry;
Bessy always had to wait,
    While Mary lived in plenty.

PLAY DAYS

How many days has my baby to
    play?
    Saturday, Sunday, Monday,
Tuesday, Wednesday, Thursday,
    Friday,
    Saturday, Sunday, Monday.

WHEN

When I was
a bachelor
I lived by
myself;
And all the
bread and
cheese I got
I laid up on the
shelf.

The rats and the mice
They made such a strife,
I was forced to go to London
To buy me a wife.

THE MOUSE AND THE CLOCK

Hickory, dickory, dock!

The mouse ran up the clock;

The clock struck one,

And down he run,

Hickory, dickory, dock!

NEEDLES AND PINS

Needles and pins, needles and pins,
When a man marries his trouble
  begins.

THE BLACK HEN

Hickety, pickety, my black hen,
She lays eggs for gentlemen;
Gentlemen come every day
To see what my black hen
    doth lay.

THE HOBBY-HORSE

I had a little hobby-horse,
    And it was dapple gray;
Its head was made of pea-straw,
    Its tail was made of hay.

I sold it to an old woman
    For a copper groat;
And I'll not sing my song again
    Without another coat.

THE BOY IN THE BARN

A little boy went into a barn,
   And lay down on some hay.
An owl came out, and flew about,
   And the little boy ran away.

THREE STRAWS

Three straws on a staff
Would make a baby cry and laugh.

OVER THE WATER

Over the water, and over the sea,
And over the water to Charley,
I'll have none of your nasty beef,
Nor I'll have none of your barley;
But I'll have some of your very best
    flour
To make a white cake for my
    Charley.

AROUND THE GREEN GRAVEL

Around the green gravel the grass
    grows green,
And all the pretty maids are plain
    to be seen;
Wash them with milk, and clothe
    them with silk,
And write their names with a pen
    and ink.

THE BLACKSMITH

"Robert Barnes, my fellow fine,
Can you shoe this horse of mine?"
"Yes, good sir, that I can,
As well as any other man;
There's a nail, and there's a prod,
Now, good sir, your horse is shod."

YOUNG LAMBS TO SELL

If I'd as much money as I could tell,
I never would cry young lambs to sell;
Young lambs to sell, young lambs to sell;
I never would cry young lambs to sell.

THE TARTS

The Queen of Hearts,
She made some tarts,
All on a summer's day;
The Knave of Hearts,
He stole the tarts,
And took them clean away.

WILLY BOY

"Willy boy, Willy boy, where are
    you going?
I will go with you, if that I
    may."
"I'm going to the meadow to
    see them a-mowing,
I'm going to help them to make
    the hay."

THE QUARREL

My little old man and I fell out;
I 'll tell you what 'twas all about, —
I had money and he had none,
And that's the way the noise begun.

LITTLE JENNY WREN

Little Jenny Wren fell sick,
    Upon a time;
In came Robin Redbreast
    And brought her cake and
    wine.

"Eat well of my cake, Jenny,
    Drink well of my wine."
"Thank you, Robin, kindly,
    You shall be mine."

Jenny she got well,
    And stood upon her feet,
And told Robin plainly
    She loved him not a bit.

Robin being angry,
    Hopped upon a twig,
Saying, "Out upon you! Fie upon
    you!
    Bold-faced jig!"

DOCTOR FOSTER

Doctor Foster went to Glo'ster,
  In a shower of rain;
He stepped in a puddle, up to his
    middle,
  And never went there again.

THREE WISE MEN OF GOTHAM

Three wise men of Gotham
Went to sea in a bowl;
If the bowl had been stronger
My song had been longer.

CRY, BABY

Cry, baby, cry,
Put your finger in your eye,
And tell your mother it wasn't I.

MY MAID MARY

My maid Mary she minds the dairy,
  While I go a-hoeing and mowing
  each morn;
Gaily run the reel and the little
  spinning wheel.
  While I am singing and mowing
  my corn.

FOREHEAD, EYES, CHEEKS, NOSE, MOUTH, AND CHIN

Here sits the Lord Mayor,
  Here sit his two men,
Here sits the cock,
  Here sits the hen,
Here sit the little chickens,
  Here they run in.
Chin-chopper, chin-chopper, chin
  chopper, chin!

THE COACHMAN

Up at Piccadilly, oh!
    The coachman takes his stand,
And when he meets a pretty girl
    He takes her by the hand;
Whip away forever, oh!
    Drive away so clever, oh!
All the way to Bristol, oh!
    He drives her four-in-hand.

SATURDAY, SUNDAY

On Saturday night
    Shall be all my care
To powder my locks
    And curl my hair.

On Sunday morning
    My love will come in,
When he will marry me
    With a gold ring.

THE LITTLE BIRD

Once I saw a little bird
    Come hop, hop, hop;
So I cried, "Little bird,
    Will you stop, stop, stop?"

And was going to the window
    To say, "How do you do?"
But he shook his little tail,
    And far away he flew.

BIRDS OF A FEATHER

Birds of a feather flock together,
    And so will pigs and swine;
Rats and mice will have their choice,
    And so will I have mine.

MY LOVE

Saw ye aught of my love a-coming
   from the market?
   A peck of meal upon her back,
   A babby in her basket;
Saw ye aught of my love a-coming
   from the market?

ELIZABETH

Elizabeth, Elspeth, Betsy, and
   Bess,
They all went together to seek a
   bird's nest;
They found a bird's nest with five
   eggs in,
They all took one, and left four in.

HUSH-A-BYE

Hush-a-bye, baby, on the tree top!
When the wind blows the cradle
    will rock;
When the bough breaks the cradle
    will fall;
Down will come baby, bough, cradle
    and all.

COME, LET'S TO BED

"To bed! To bed!"
  Says Sleepy-head;
"Tarry awhile," says Slow;
"Put on the pan,"
  Says Greedy Nan;
  "We'll sup before we go."

OLD GRIMES

Old Grimes is dead, that good old
man,
We ne'er shall see him more;
He used to wear a long brown coat
All buttoned down before.

CANDLE-SAVING

To make your candles last for aye,
You wives and maids give ear-O!
To put them out's the only way,
Says honest John Boldero.

HUSH-A-BYE

Hush-a-bye, baby, lie still with thy
    daddy,
    Thy mammy has gone to the
    mill,
To get some meal to bake a cake,
    So pray, my dear baby, lie still.

ROCK-A-BYE, BABY

Rock-a-bye, baby, thy cradle is green;
Father's a nobleman, mother's a
    queen;
And Betty's a lady, and wears a
    gold ring;
And Johnny's a drummer, and
    drums for the king.

HUSH-A-BYE

Hush-a-bye, baby,
    Daddy is near;
Mamma is a lady,
    And that's very clear.

THE MAN OF TOBAGO

There was an old man of Tobago
Who lived on rice, gruel, and sago,
Till much to his bliss,
His physician said this:
"To a leg, sir, of mutton, you may
go."

WEE WILLIE WINKIE

Wee Willie Winkie runs through
the town,

Upstairs and downstairs, in his
nightgown;

Rapping at the window, crying
through the lock,

"Are the children in their beds?
Now it's eight o'clock."

LITTLE FRED

When little Fred went to bed,
    He always said his prayers;
He kissed mamma, and then papa,
    And straightway went upstairs.

SLEEP, BABY, SLEEP

Sleep, baby, sleep,
Our cottage vale is deep:
The little lamb is on the green,
With woolly fleece so soft and clean
Sleep, baby, sleep.

A CANDLE

Little Nanny Etticoat
In a white petticoat,
And a red nose;
The longer she stands
The shorter she grows.

BEDTIME

The Man in the Moon looked
    out of the moon,
  Looked out of the moon
    and said,
"'Tis time for all children
    on the earth
    To think about getting to bed!"

JACK

Jack be nimble, Jack be
quick,

Jack jump over the candle-
stick.